Rocky Rocks and
The Colourful Socks

Seniha Slowinski

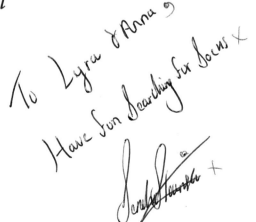

Clink
Street

London | New York

Published by Clink Street Publishing 2017

Copyright © 2017

illustrations by Nick Roberts

First edition.

ISBNs: 978-1-912262-27-4 paperback
978-1-912262-28-1 ebook

Acknowledgements

Rocky Rocks and the Colourful Socks was initially inspired by my dog Rocky and the children that I taught at Arnott Pre School, Thamesmead.

I'd like to thank Kaan and Thema Fehmi and their two beautiful children Saba and Turkan for their continued support. My dear friend Vesna Andrews, thank you for always believing in me. Melek, Cengiz, and Meliz Kerim, thank you for all the laughter and joy you brought me whilst creating the Rocky Rocks books. Tony Murray, my deepest gratitude for your generosity. To my niece and nephew, Peri and Kenan Coban, my two favourite people, I can not thank you enough for being my little guinea pigs and always allowing me to read my books to you both.

Seniha Slowinski

Hello!
My name is Rocky Rocks
I like to play with colourful socks

I like to play a game called hide and seek
Where I can look for socks wherever I peek
Would you like to play with me?
We will have fun
And I would love your company

In the kitchen is a good place to start
Can you see the sock next to the apple tart?
'If you can see' you must tell me
What colour sock you can see?
I will give you a clue; it rhymes with bean
Could it be the colour…

In the bedroom now we shall go
Can you see the sock by my Daddy's big toe?
'If you can see' you must tell me
What colour sock you can see?
I will give you a clue; it rhymes with bed
Could it be the colour…

In the living room, under the couch, a sock is hiding
Do you think you can find it?
'If you can see' you must tell me
What colour sock you can see?
I will give you a clue; it rhymes with chew
Could it be the colour…

Off we go in to the bathroom
Can you see the sock next to the broom?
'If you can see' you must tell me
What colour sock you can see?
I will give you a clue; it rhymes with fellow
Could it be the colour…

In the basement under the house
I can see a sock by my friend Mr Mouse
'If you can see' you must tell me
What colour sock you can see?
I will give you a clue; it rhymes with flight
Could it be the colour...

Outside the house and in the garage
A sock is hanging on Mummy's collage
'If you can see' you must tell me
What colour sock you can see?
I will give you a clue; it rhymes with stink
Could it be the colour…

In the dining room on the grandfather clock
I think I can a see a little sock
'If you can see' you must tell me
What colour sock you can see?
I will give you a clue; it rhymes with turtle
Could it be the colour...

Out in the garden and into the shed
A sock is sitting with Mr Ted
'If you can see' you must tell me
What colour sock you can see
I will give you a clue; it rhymes with porridge
Could it be the colour…

There are no more socks to be found
But you played so well and have made me SO proud
To have friends like you to play with me
Makes me so happy; I scream yippeeee!
I hope to play with you again
Until then
This is…

The Real Rocky!

Photography by Michael Kabourakis
Instagram: mkabourakisphotography

Lightning Source UK Ltd.
Milton Keynes UK
UKHW050221220119
335949UK00001B/4/P